# LITTLE big Insects

## Perm Worm and a Different Day

ISBN 978 1838595 258

British Library Cataloguing in Publication Data.
A catalogue record for this book is available from the British Library.

Typeset in 20pt Tovari Sans by Troubador Publishing Ltd, Leicester, UK

Matador is an imprint of Troubador Publishing Ltd

For the Hilarious Hollie and the Open-hearted Olivia,
your originality will always be your strength.
And to the many children I have had the privilege to
meet throughout my career.
You have all inspired and guided my writing.
You are all unique and utterly amazing!

In an enormous universe

On a humongous planet

In a gigantic country

In a massive city

In a big, big garden

Lived the LITTLE big insects, each unique
and each AMAZINGLY POWERFUL!

This story takes us on an adventure
of discovery with Perm Worm.

Perm Worm lives with his family in an underground hole.

Every day has to be the same for Perm Worm.

He gets out of bed at precisely 6.30am,
always puts his sock on first before anything
else, which always has to be rolled
down three times.

He listens to his favourite song 'In the soil' by the
Wormicles, always before breakfast!

At breakfast he has the same bowl of vegetable scraps every day, in the same bowl with the same matching spoon, sitting on the same chair.

Perm Worm arrives at Grassroutes school at precisely 8.45am. His teacher, Sweetle Beetle, greets him at the door every day.

Perm Worm loves learning about space and planets. He knows the names of all the planets and exactly how big they are; he even knows how hot they are too!

He knows many, many facts about space he could talk for hours and hours about all he knows.

One thing Perm Worm doesn't know
much about are other insects.

He finds making friends difficult; he doesn't
understand other insects, he doesn't know when to
laugh with them or when to ask if they are OK.

He finds it even harder to listen to them
and not want to talk about space!

He does have one special friend who
understands him and that is Clicket Cricket;
they have been friends since Perm Worm
and Clicket Cricket were baby insects.

One day, Perm Worm's whole world changed.
This was just awful for Perm Worm as he
does not like anything to change!

Perm Worm got up at the same time,
put his sock on the same, had the same breakfast
and arrived at school at the same time.

But suddenly Perm Worm felt a funny feeling creep
over him. He wanted to hide in the soil! As where once
stood his kind, loving teacher, Sweetle Beetle, now
stood a new face, one he had not seen before.

He'd had no warning of this change, no idea,
no clue — who was this insect?

Where was his teacher? Why was she not in her
usual place at 8.45am? He had done everything the
same, so why were things different?

"Hello Perm Worm," came a jovial voice.
"My name is Mr Cough Moth." At that very moment,
Mr Cough Moth coughed and flew straight into a
lightbulb. Then he coughed again and flew into the
same lightbulb! And he did it again and again!

"Ahmmm hmmm, sorry about that," said Mr Cough
Moth, as he dusted himself down. "Can't seem to stop
it! Aaaaanyway, where was I... OH YES, I am your new
teacher," Mr Cough Moth introduced himself.

Perm Worm said nothing, but he didn't like this one bit!

He found he couldn't listen or concentrate
in class that day, he couldn't eat his lunch,
he just wanted to go home.

When he got home, all the feelings that he had kept inside all day came out with a big bang.

He shouted at his mummy, "GO AWAY!"

He shouted at his daddy, when his daddy asked him what was wrong. "STOP TALKING TO ME!"

He stamped his tail and slammed his door!

The next day arrived but Perm Worm wouldn't get up.

He wouldn't put his sock on and he
wouldn't eat his breakfast.

Eventually he arrived in school but he was late.

Perm Worm saw his mummy talking to Mr Cough Moth.

Later that day, Mr Cough Moth sat down next to Perm
Worm; he gave him some cards with funny faces on.

One had a face that looked cross and
one had a face with its mouth open, which Mr Cough
Moth explained was an insect laughing. One of the
cards had a picture of an insect crying on it.

Mr Cough Moth told Perm Worm that these
cards could help him show how he feels, if he is
struggling to talk about his feelings.

Mr Cough Moth also explained to Perm Worm that Sweetle Beetle would be back soon and Mr Cough Moth would be there to help him until then.

Perm Worm had never known how to tell other insects how he feels, but he liked these cards, even though they were different.

So, in the end, Perm Worm did have a different day and he may have many more different days to come. But he learned that there are always ways to cope with changes and his family and people who love him will help him through it, no matter what.

For exclusive discounts on Matador titles,
sign up to our occasional newsletter at
troubador.co.uk/bookshop